The Good Times Book

By Dawn McMillan

Illustrated by Annie White

Chapter 1

The Accident

Mum turned the car into the street where Harry's great-grandad lived.

"Mum!" shouted Harry. "There's an ambulance outside Pop's house! What's happening?"

"Oh no!" whispered Mum anxiously. "I wonder what the trouble is."

Mum parked the car near Pop's driveway, and she and Harry ran to the house. The ambulance officers were bringing Pop out through the door on a stretcher. Harry could see Pop's face, pale with shock.

Pop tried to smile. "Don't worry," he said with a little groan. "I'll be all right. I fell over in the kitchen and I've hurt my leg."

"His leg's broken," one of the ambulance officers explained. "We're taking him to hospital."

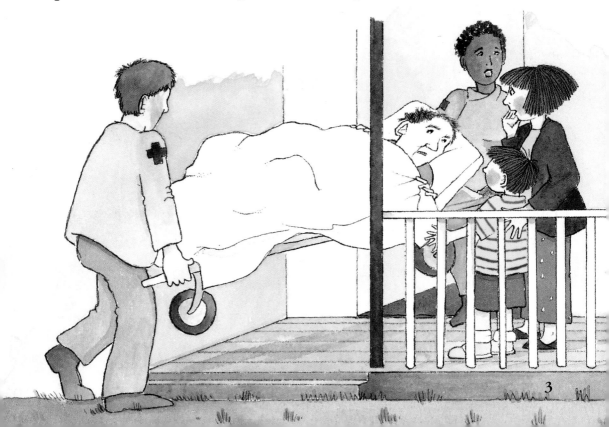

Chapter 2

Where Will Pop Live?

Mum and Harry followed the ambulance to the hospital. They waited while the doctors looked at Pop's leg. Finally, the nurses put Pop into a bed, and then Harry and Mum sat down beside him.

Pop looked very old, and Harry was afraid.

"I'll be better tomorrow, after the doctors operate on my leg," Pop whispered.

"Will that hurt?" Harry asked anxiously.

Mum looked at Harry and said quickly, "They'll put Pop to sleep, and it'll be all over before he wakes up."

Mum and Harry went back to see Pop the day after his operation. Harry was surprised to see him awake and smiling.

"It's good to see you both," Pop said cheerfully. "The doctors say I'll be able to walk again soon."

"That's a relief!" Mum replied.

Pop reached for Mum's hand and said, "But I can't live by myself now. I realise that it's too dangerous to be alone at my age."

Harry turned to Mum. "Can Pop live with us?" he asked. "Please, Mum?"

"Of course he can!" Mum answered.

But Pop spoke up quickly. "No, thank you," he said. "I love you both very much, but I've decided to live in the rest home. My friend Jimmy lives there, and I'll enjoy being with people my own age."

"What's a rest home?" asked Harry, still worried.

"It's a place where old people live together and get special care," Pop answered. "I'm excited about the rest home, but I'm sad about having to sell my house. However, I just have to accept that the time is right for me to move out."

"Are you sure, Pop?" Harry asked thoughtfully.

"I'm quite sure!" Pop answered.

Chapter 3

The 'Good Times' Book

The first time Mum and Harry went to see Pop at the rest home he was in his bedroom, sitting in his favourite green chair, which he'd brought from his old house.

Harry looked around. "This room is so tiny!" he whispered, remembering how big Pop's old house had been.

"Don't worry, Harry," Pop said. "It's all I need. We all share a big lounge, and we have our dinner together. Everyone is very friendly here, so it's fun doing things together," he smiled.

When Harry got home, he looked out of his bedroom window. Through the trees he could see the rooftop of Pop's house. He remembered all the good times he'd had there and he felt upset. "Now someone else will live there," he muttered.

Suddenly he had an idea. He hurried downstairs to Mum and said, "Let's make Pop a 'Good Times' book! I'll paint a picture of his house for the cover, and we can fill the book with photos!"

After dinner, Mum and Harry looked through a box of photos together. "There are so many to choose from!" Mum smiled. "I like this one of Pop's garden, with the huge pumpkin!"

"Let's use this one!" Harry suggested as he reached for a photo of Pop falling into a swimming pool. "He made a *gigantic* splash, like a whale!"

Harry looked at more photos. "He'll probably like the family ones best," he said, and Mum agreed.

"Remember his birthday party?" Harry laughed. "And his cake with the candles that wouldn't blow out!"

Chapter 4

The Surprise

The next day, when they had finished the book, Harry and Mum went to the rest home to visit Pop.

"He's in the lounge with Jimmy," said a nurse. "Those two never stop talking!"

When Pop saw Harry he called out excitedly, "Hello, Harry! Come and meet my friend Jimmy. He's been telling me all about the fun times he had when he was younger."

Harry held the 'Good Times' book behind his back. "We've got something special for you, Pop," he said. Then he held out the book and said, "We've made a book about *your* fun times!"

Pop reached out, took the book carefully, and put it on the table. "My house!" he whispered as he looked at the cover. "You've painted a picture of my house! Thank you, Harry!"

"Look inside, Pop!" said Harry impatiently.

Pop turned the pages slowly. In silence he looked at all the photos, and then with a tremble in his voice he said, "This is a wonderful gift!"

Pop closed the book gently, looked up at Mum and Harry and said, "We've sure had some good times!"

Harry gave Pop a hug and said, "I love you, Pop! We'll do lots more fun things together, and then I'll make you *another* book."